W9-BWB-574

Good Luck
Charlie

Written by Jennifer E. Kramer   Illustrated by Jeff Moores

Children's Press®
A Division of Scholastic Inc.
New York • Toronto • London • Auckland • Sydney
Mexico City • New Delhi • Hong Kong
Danbury, Connecticut

*To my husband and inspiration, Andrew, and my "four" lucky charms,
Mitchell, Patrick, Jessica, and Baby Kramer*
—J.E.K.

To Charlie and Sammy
—J.M.

Reading Consultants

Linda Cornwell
Literacy Specialist

Katharine A. Kane
Education Consultant
(Retired, San Diego County Office of Education and
San Diego State University)

Library of Congress Cataloging-in-Publication Data
Kramer, Jennifer E.
  Good luck, Charlie / written by Jennifer E. Kramer ; illustrated by Jeff Moores.
    p. cm. — (A Rookie reader)
  Summary: Charlie tries to use lucky charms to win a baseball game, but
  all he really needs is his lucky pitching arm.
    ISBN 0-516-21722-4 (lib. bdg.)   0-516-25826-5 (pbk.)
    [1. Baseball—Fiction. 2. Luck—Fiction. 3. Stories in rhyme.] I.Moores, Jeff, ill.
  II. Title. III. Series.
  PZ8.3.K8625 Go 2004
  [E]—dc22
                                      2003018658

CHILDREN'S PRESS, and A ROOKIE READER®, and associated logos are trademarks
and or registered trademarks of Scholastic Library Publishing. SCHOLASTIC and associated
logos are trademarks and or registered trademarks of Scholastic Inc.
1 2 3 4 5 6 7 8 9 10 R 13 12 11 10 09 08 07 06 05 04

The game is just about to start.
"Good luck, Charlie, do your part!"

His friend Pete is up at bat.
Charlie tips his lucky hat.

"Strike one!"

7

"We need a hit. We don't have many!"
Charlie rubs his lucky penny.

"Strike two!"

The game is close. It's nearly over.
Charlie twirls his lucky clover.

12

"Strike three!"

15

"The other team is up," says Pete.
"Hurry, Charlie, on your feet!"

18

	1	2	3	4	5	6	
	3	0	2	0	1	0	6
	0	1	3	1	2		7

"We lead by one. No time to rest."
"Good luck, Charlie, do your best!"

Charlie runs in past the gate.
The batter steps up to home plate.

The final inning. This is it.
The batter swings. "Oh no, a hit!"

Charlie nods. He'll pitch once more.
One man on third. He must not score.

25

The ball flies fast. Pete gives a shout.
The batter missed. Three strikes.
They're OUT!

Three outs. No runs. Their time has passed.
Charlie's team has won, at last.

	1	2	3	4	5	6
	3	0	2	0	1	0	6
	0	1	3	1	2		7

"Charlie, keep your lucky charms."
"We just need your lucky arms!"

Word List (97 words)

a	friend	keep	out	swings
about	game	last	outs	team
arms	gate	lead	over	the
at	gives	luck	part	their
ball	good	lucky	passed	they're
bat	has	man	past	third
batter	hat	many	penny	this
best	have	missed	Pete	three
by	he	more	pitch	time
Charlie	he'll	must	plate	tips
Charlie's	his	nearly	rest	to
charms	hit	need	rubs	twirls
close	home	no	runs	two
clover	hurry	nods	says	up
do	in	not	score	we
don't	inning	oh	shout	won
fast	is	on	start	your
feet	it	once	steps	
final	it's	one	strike	
flies	just	other	strikes	

About the Author

Jennifer E. Kramer believes that a love of reading is one of the greatest gifts you can give a child. She has written and published several children's stories, one of which recently appeared in *Highlights for Children*.

About the Illustrator

Jeff Moores lives in the Finger Lakes Region of New York State. Ever since Jeff was a little, goofy boy, he liked to draw little, goofy characters. Now his humorous characters can be see in major publications, television commercials, and web sites. Jeff also loves to bring his characters to life through animation.